Scholastic Children's Books
An imprint of Scholastic Ltd
Euston House, 24 Eversholt Street, London, NW1 1DB, UK
Registered office: Westfield Road, Southam, Warwickshire, CV47 0RA
SCHOLASTIC and associated logos are trademarks and/or
registered trademarks of Scholastic Inc.

First published in the UK by Scholastic Ltd, 2017

Text copyright © Paula Harrison, 2017
Cover illustration copyright © Hatem Aly, in the style of Michelle
Ouelette, represented by The Bright Agency, 2017
Inside illustration copyright © Hatem Aly, in the style of Michelle
Ouelette, represented by The Bright Agency, 2017

The right of Paula Harrison and Hatem Aly to be identified as the author
and illustrator of this work has been asserted by them.

Trade ISBN 978 1407 17080 0
Book Club ISBN 978 1407 17432 7

A CIP catalogue record for this book
is available from the British Library.

Printed by CPI Group (UK) Ltd, Croydon, CR0 4YY

Papers used by Scholastic Children's Books are made
from wood grown in sustainable forests.

1 3 5 7 9 10 8 6 4 2

This is a work of fiction. Names, characters, places, incidents
and dialogues are products of the author's imagination or are used
fictitiously. Any resemblance to actual people, living or dead,
events or locales is entirely coincidental.

www.scholastic.co.uk

The Hunt for Hidden Treasure

Paula Harrison

SCHOLASTIC

For John and Pauline

Chapter One

The Artist of Bodkin Street

Jess dashed up the back stairs of Peveril Palace. Her white apron was smudged with sooty fingerprints and her mob cap was falling over one ear. She knocked on the door to Princess Amelia's chamber before bursting in.

"Millie!" she gasped. "Your mother sent me to fetch you. The carriage is waiting to take you to Plumchester."

Princess Amelia (called Millie, for short) swung round, holding one hand to her neck. The two girls were the same age and they looked so much alike that they could have been twins. They both had glossy brown hair that curled over their shoulders, small noses and hazel eyes. The only difference between them was that Jess's eyes were a little darker.

They'd been best friends ever since Jess came to Peveril Palace to work as a maid. They loved looking the same and they secretly called themselves Double Trouble!

"I can't go to Plumchester!" cried Millie. "Mother wants me to have my portrait painted by that new artist in Bodkin Street."

"Don't you want to have your picture painted?" asked Jess.

"It's not that – look!" Millie took her hand away from her neck and showed Jess a bright yellow stain across her skin. "I put on face paints last night – I was pretending to be a lion in the jungle. I washed most of it off before I went to bed but I must have missed this bit and now I can't get rid of it. Mother will be so cross! She warned me not to make a mess."

Jess grinned. "I bet you looked great as a lion. Can't you put on a silk scarf to hide the mark?"

"I know Mother won't let me. She's already decided exactly what I should wear. The portrait's going to be a present for Grandmother in Glenbarr so it has to be perfect." Millie pulled a face.

"Why don't we swap places? I'll get my picture painted and you can finish my chores. No one will ever know!" Jess's eyes twinkled. She and Millie swapped places all the time so that they could both do their favourite things. Jess would go to Millie's horse-riding lesson while Millie went to the palace kitchen to bake cakes with Cook Walsh. It was pretty awesome to be a maid and a princess all in one day!

Millie clapped her hands excitedly. "I'd love to swap! But are you sure you don't mind?"

Jess grinned. "Course not! We'd better hurry though. What do I have to wear?"

Millie went to her big wooden wardrobe and took out a long purple dress with sparkly beads all over the top and a silver sash around the waist. Jess took off her maid uniform and gave it to Millie, before pulling the dress over her white petticoat.

Millie put the maid dress on and fastened the apron round her waist. Then she brushed Jess's long hair until it hung beautifully over her shoulders before clipping an emerald necklace round her friend's neck.

Jess gazed into the large gold-framed mirror and her heart skipped. She was used to wearing royal clothes but this was one of Millie's finest dresses which was only worn on very special occasions.

"You look great!" Millie beamed. "Are you all right? Is the dress too scratchy?"

"It's fine! You'd better take this." Jess picked up her mob cap and put it on Millie's head. "I hope Mr Steen doesn't give you too many chores."

"Don't worry about me—" Millie broke off at the sound of footsteps.

There was a sharp knock on the door. "Come in!" the girls called together.

Mr Steen, the royal butler, opened the door, his eyebrows lowered in disapproval. "You were meant to fetch the princess right away, Jess," he said to Millie. "The royal carriage is waiting."

"Sorry, Mr Steen." Millie turned away to hide a giggle.

"Here!" Jess handed her friend a gauzy white scarf and stared meaningfully at the stain on Millie's skin. "This will keep your neck warm."

"Oh! Thank you." Millie wrapped it

6

round her neck to hide the yellow mark.

Jess felt a fluttering in her stomach as she followed the butler downstairs. Riding out in the royal carriage wearing a special dress and an emerald necklace seemed very daring. As she sat down in the carriage, she noticed one of the gardeners leaning on his spade and staring through a window into the banquet hall.

Just then Mr Larum, Millie's teacher, rushed down the steps carrying a large package wrapped in brown paper and string. "I'm ready!" he gasped as he climbed into the carriage. "And I've got the royal paintings."

"You there!" Mr Steen spotted the gardener leaning on his spade. "You're new here, aren't you? Aren't there some flower beds that need digging?"

"Yes, sir. I'm sorry." The gardener pulled

his straw hat down low and hurried away.

The coachman called to the horses and the carriage rolled forward. Jess watched the royal lake and the golden palace gates go by. Then they were rumbling down the street towards the city of Plumchester.

Mr Larum sat opposite Jess holding the wrapped-up paintings carefully. King James had noticed their frames needed mending so he'd asked Mr Larum to take them to the artist in Bodkin Street who would surely know how to fix them.

"There is such a lot of history behind these paintings," said Mr Larum, straightening his dark-rimmed glasses. "They were painted more than a hundred years ago during the reign of King Ned, your great-grandfather."

Jess smiled and tried to listen but there were so many exciting things outside the window. Street sellers were setting out

stalls with everything from fruit to feather hats. Halfpenny Square, where the biggest market was held, was filling with people and noise.

As the carriage rolled along, Jess tried to remember one thing about each person she saw – the lace on a lady's sleeves or the colour of a man's coat. It was something she'd been practising in case it came in handy for solving mysteries.

She and Millie had solved quite a few puzzles lately. It had all begun when Prince Edward's little diamond crown went missing right before his first birthday. The two girls had searched for clues and found the crown. Jess couldn't help wondering whether there was another mystery out there, waiting to be discovered.

At last, the carriage turned left and drew to a stop in Bodkin Street. Jess flung the carriage door open and jumped down, quite forgetting to let the coachman open it for her like a princess should. She loved Bodkin Street. She'd lived here in her parents' dressmaking shop, Buttons and Bows, before becoming a maid at the palace. She knew every house and shop in the lane, except the exciting new artist's studio.

Smiling, she waved to Miss Clackton, the kind but scatty owner of the Pet Emporium next door to her parents' shop. The Pet Emporium was a place for pampering pets and was filled with every kind of animal toy and treat Jess could think of.

The wonderful smell of freshly baked cakes drifted out of Mr Bibby's bakery just across the road. Next door to the bakery was the ironmonger's and Mr Heddon, who ran the shop, was sweeping the doorstep.

"This way, Princess Amelia." The

coachman beckoned her towards a bright red front door. *Gilbert Small's Studio* was painted in gold letters on a sign above the window.

Jess stepped forward eagerly. Mr Gilbert Small was the only person in Bodkin Street that she'd never met. It was only two weeks since he'd moved in and set up his artist studio and this was Jess's first chance to look inside! A proper painter like Mr Small must be very serious and probably frowned a lot while trying to get his pictures just right.

The coachman held the door and Mr Larum staggered inside with his package of paintings. Following him, Jess gazed around with wide eyes. Tall trees with dangling tropical fruit were painted across the walls. Pictures of birds with bright feathers and monkeys with furry faces peeped from the painted branches. Dazzling flowers in magenta, gold and crimson were drawn on the forest floor. Overhead, the ceiling was a beautiful shade of blue.

Jess caught her breath. It was like stepping into a jungle.

"Welcome, welcome!" boomed a large man with ginger hair and a beard. He shook Mr Larum's hand. "Nice to see you, sir! And this must be the princess."

"Hello!" Jess tried not to stare as she curtsied. How could someone called Mr Small be so enormous? He was like a ginger-haired giant.

Mr Larum unwrapped the parcel of paintings and began talking to Gilbert Small about the repairs, so Jess looked around the room. Paintings of places and people were stacked against the walls. Beside a large easel was a chair with a sleepy ginger cat lying on it. Jess peeked at the paper on the easel but it was blank.

"I'll let you get on." Mr Larum shook the artist's hand again. "I'll be back with the carriage at midday."

Mr Small stacked the royal pictures that Mr Larum had brought carefully to one side. Then he stroked the sleeping ginger cat. "Rumble-tum! You're sitting on the young lady's chair. This is Rumble-tum," he told Jess. "I gave him that name because he purrs so loudly."

Rumble-tum yawned and stretched, before climbing down.

"Will it take you long to paint me, Mr Small?" Jess asked timidly as she sat down on the chair.

"Call me Gilbert!" he boomed, lines creasing round his eyes as he smiled. "No, it won't take too long. Now sit as comfortably as you can and I'll start the picture."

Jess tried to sit very still but she jumped

when Rumble-tum sprang on to her knees. She stroked the cat's fluffy ginger ears and he curled up on her lap, purring loudly. Jess smiled. "I think Rumble-tum wants to be in the picture too!"

Chapter Two

The Runaway Cheese

Gilbert Small made lots of little marks with his pencil and stopped to look up at Jess every now and then.

After a few minutes, Miss Clackton burst in with a kitten in one hand and a paper bag full of iced buns in the other. Her straggly hair was escaping from a hair clip and her dress was covered with bird seeds.

"Yoo hoo!" She beamed at Jess. "Are you having your picture painted? I've brought Fluffy to meet Rumble-tum. I think they're going to be great friends!" She dropped the kitten into Jess's lap next to the ginger cat. Rumble-tum gave the kitten a lick and then went back to sleep again.

Soon more passers-by came in. There were two ladies wearing velvet jackets, an old man with a limp and a young man with a tall grey hat. Everyone stopped to admire Gilbert's picture even though he'd only drawn Jess's mouth and nose.

Gilbert chuckled and put down his pencil. "Let's stop for a little while," he said to Jess. "I'll set the kettle to boil and mend those picture frames for the king." He spread out the paintings Mr Larum had brought on a table.

"These are wonderful!" Miss Clackton peered at the pictures. "Just look at that adorable cat!"

Jess carefully set Rumble-tum and the kitten down, and went over to look. The largest picture was of the palace and royal garden. The three smaller ones showed places in Plumchester – Halfpenny Square,

St Anne's church and the soldiers' garrison. There was a black cat with sparkling green eyes in each of the smaller paintings.

"These pictures were painted by the great artist Arthur Black. See, there's his name." Gilbert pointed to a squiggle in the corner of the paintings. "They're worth an awful lot of money."

"We'd better keep an eye on them then!" said Miss Clackton, with a laugh. "We don't want anyone running away with the king's most valuable pictures."

The other customers came closer to look at the royal paintings before Gilbert took them into the back room to fix the frames. Miss Clackton handed out the buns which were topped with soft white icing.

At last, Miss Clackton and the customers left and Gilbert worked on his picture of Jess. He finished sketching with his pencil and began painting her dress and hair. He stopped now and then to give Jess some drawing tips. He even showed her how to mix the paints together.

"So blue and red make purple." Jess mixed the blobs of paint together and swirled them round and round on the palette. "This is so much fun!"

"I'm afraid it's time to go," said Mr Larum, who had just come in.

"Shall I come back tomorrow?" said Jess, eagerly. "You need to finish my picture, don't you? Could I bring my friend too? She likes to draw and I know she'd love it here."

Gilbert smiled. "Your friend is very welcome. I'll even let you add some animals to the jungle on my wall."

"That would be amazing!" gasped Jess.

Gilbert wrapped up the royal paintings and handed them back to Mr Larum. His eyes twinkled as he shook Jess's hand and said goodbye.

Jess gazed out of the carriage window on the way home. She had so much to tell Millie! She knew her friend would love Rumble-tum. Millie loved animals and there were no cats at Peveril Palace, just Jax their crazy but lovable golden cocker spaniel.

The carriage rattled past Halfpenny Square and carried on towards the palace. Mr Larum held tight to the wrapped–up paintings. Suddenly the carriage slowed down.

"Hey! Is anyone there?" shouted the coachman.

They came to a stop and there was a thud as the coachman climbed down from his box.

"What on earth is he doing?" cried Mr Larum. "I don't want to wait around. I have things to do back at the palace."

Jess peered through the window. A cart full of large circles of cheese was blocking the road ahead. Its back was open and the cheese was rolling down the wooden ramp and spilling out on to the street.

"I don't think we can get past," said Jess. "There's cheese on the road!"

"Cheese? That's ridiculous!" Mr Larum laid the paintings on the seat and leaned out the window, calling, "Hello there! Can anyone move that cheese? We've got to get back to the palace."

"I'm doing my best, sir!" called the coachman. "But there doesn't seem to be anyone in charge of this cart."

"Dear me!" Mr Larum climbed out and began giving the coachman instructions.

Jess scrambled down too and managed to push three cheeses back into the cart. Each one was the size of a small wheel. They were really heavy and had a very strong smell. Some had escaped, rolling right down the hill towards the river.

"Your Highness! You mustn't do that," exclaimed Mr Larum. "You might get that lovely dress dirty." He opened the carriage door and tried to usher Jess back inside.

Jess was just about to argue that she didn't mind getting dirty when she caught sight of some ripped brown paper on the carriage seat. Darting up the steps, she grabbed the shreds of paper that the paintings had been wrapped in.

One painting still lay on the seat. But there had been four of them before!

A horrible cold feeling grew in her tummy. "Mr Larum! Some of the paintings are gone!"

"They can't be! I counted them when we left Mr Small's studio. They're all wrapped up in paper." Mr Larum followed Jess into the carriage and his face went white. "Oh my goodness! Someone's taken them. Some scoundrel came in here while we weren't looking." Dashing down the steps, he called to the coachman for help.

Jess jumped out. Was there someone running away with a stack of paintings under their arm? She shaded her eyes and looked up and down the road. No one nearby looked suspicious. No one was carrying paintings under their arm.

"King James will be so cross!" Mr Larum took off his round glasses and wiped them. "Three royal paintings stolen! Who would dare do such a thing right in front of us? We're lucky the thief didn't take them all."

Jess looked at the painting lying on the carriage seat. It was the largest picture – the one of the palace and royal garden. The three smaller paintings – the ones with the little black cat – were gone.

Chapter Three

The Picture Left Behind

As soon as Millie heard the news about the missing paintings, she grabbed a feather duster and hurried off to find Jess. Being a maid for the whole morning had been fun. She'd done some chores for Mr Steen, but she'd also helped Cook Walsh make a cake and played with her dog, Jax, in the garden.

She wondered what had happened in Plumchester. Surely Mr Larum hadn't been careless enough to lose the royal paintings?

Mr Steen, the butler, passed her halfway up the palace stairs. As usual, his dark hair was neat and there wasn't a speck of dust on his black suit. "Have you finished polishing *all* the silverware in the banquet hall?"

"Yes, sir," said Millie.

The butler raised one eyebrow. "And did you make sure everything looked perfect?"

"Um ... I think so." Millie tried to remember how good her polishing had been. She'd been daydreaming about collecting clues and solving mysteries at the time so she wasn't completely sure.

"Well, don't be long with the dusting. There's still plenty to do." Mr Steen walked stiffly down the stairs.

Millie rushed to her chamber, remembering to knock on the door as if she was Jess.

Jess flung the door open. "Millie! You'll never guess what happened!"

"Shh!" Millie rushed in, giggling. "You're supposed to be me, remember! Someone might hear you."

"Oh, I forgot!" Jess sat down on Millie's bed and stroked Jax, who was lying there snoozing. "I've got so much to tell you."

Millie listened to Jess's tale, all about the cheese and the disappearing paintings.

"No one knows who took them," finished Jess. "And that means we have a mystery to solve! I haven't got any clues so far though. I didn't see anyone suspicious."

"So the cheese cart blocked the street," said Millie. "And when you got out of the carriage the pictures were left alone."

Jess nodded. "The thief must have been really fast. I only left the carriage for a minute."

"Do you think someone put the cart there on purpose to *make* the carriage stop?" Millie looked thoughtful.

"I don't know," said Jess. "I hadn't thought of that."

Millie paced up and down the room, questions spinning round her head. Who would want the royal paintings? Had the thief planned to steal them or had he seen them in the carriage and decided right then that he wanted them? "Were the pictures wrapped up in paper while you were riding in the carriage?" she asked Jess.

"Yes, someone tore the paper off. They took three paintings – the ones with the black cat. The fourth painting was left behind."

"Paintings with a black cat... I know the ones you mean! They hung on the wall in the banquet hall. I liked those pictures," cried Millie. "Cats are so adorable!"

Jax opened his eyes and barked.

Millie laughed. "Don't worry, Jax! You're adorable too!" She paced up and down the room again. Stopping suddenly, her eyes lit up. "But if the paintings were wrapped in paper, the thief couldn't have just seen them by chance and then decided to take them. It MUST have been planned – blocking the road with the cheese and everything!"

"I guess so! The paintings were only unwrapped in the shop..." Jess bit her lip.

"What is it?" prompted Millie. "Have you remembered something?"

"Well, there were lots of people in the studio and Gilbert – the artist – started talking about the pictures. He said they were painted by a famous painter and worth an awful lot of money. Lots of people heard him!"

Millie's heart skipped. "Then that's

an important clue! Let me find my clue notebook." She dashed over to her dressing table and took a notebook and a pencil out of a drawer. Opening it up, she flicked past pages of writing and a very odd drawing of a lake monster.

Missing — three royal paintings, she wrote in big curly letters. *They are pictures of Plumchester and all of them have a black cat.*

She nibbled the end of the pencil. "Do you remember what the people in the shop looked like?"

Jess screwed up her face. "There were quite a few people. I was there and so was Gilbert Small, the artist, and Miss Clackton came in too. Then there were two ladies in velvet jackets, an old man who couldn't walk very well and another man with a grey hat. I think that's everybody."

Millie wrote it all down.

"And the two ladies were smiling and talking to each other so I think they must have been friends," added Jess.

"Brilliant!" Millie finished scribbling. "Now we just need to go to Plumchester, find them all and work out which one is the robber."

Millie and Jess swapped clothes again before going downstairs for lunch. Then Mr Larum called Millie to the schoolroom to do some spelling practice. After spellings he taught her some geography and by the time she'd learned the names of all the rivers in the kingdom, the afternoon was gone and it was too late to go to Plumchester.

At dinner time that evening, Millie pushed her spoon round and round her bowl of vegetable soup wondering where the missing paintings might be.

"Amelia, I think it's time you stopped stirring that soup and began eating it," said Queen Belinda, gently.

"Sorry I'm late, Your Majesties." Mr Larum clomped in, carrying a painting of the palace. "I wanted to show you the only picture that wasn't stolen this morning. I apologize for the loss of the smaller paintings. I blame myself—"

"Don't worry, Mr Larum," said the queen at once. "We know it wasn't your fault. You were distracted by the obstacles in the street."

"That's very kind," said Mr Larum, sadly. "But it's so embarrassing to be outwitted with cheese."

Millie managed not to giggle.

"It's odd that the largest and most expensive picture was left behind," said King James. "If the thief wanted money he

would have made more from selling that big one than all the smaller ones put together."

Millie's ears pricked up. Why *had* the thief left the largest picture? Had it been too big to carry? Jess came past with a jug of water which she set down on the banquet table. The girls exchanged looks and Millie knew Jess was wondering the same thing.

"Of course, the little pictures do have an interesting history." Mr Larum gave the picture to the butler and sat down at the table. "They were painted for King Ned a long time ago. There's even a funny old story about one of the pictures having a clue painted into it."

Millie dropped her spoon and it clattered to the floor. "A CLUE! What kind of clue?"

"Amelia, what's got into you?" chided her mother. "Mr Steen, could you bring her another spoon, please?"

Millie dived below the table to grab the spoon, sitting up again so quickly that the room spun a little. "Sorry, Mr Larum," she said, trying to hide her excitement. "Did you say there was an old story about those paintings?"

"It's nothing, really!" Mr Larum took a bite of his bread roll and chewed slowly. Millie could hardly breathe while she waited for him to answer. "Well ... there's a book about the history of Plumchester in the royal library. It says one of those paintings might reveal some treasure that got hidden away a long time ago. It's all nonsense though! No real historian would take it seriously."

Millie's eyes widened. "What kind of treasure? And how does the painting show where it is?"

"That's enough now! Let Mr Larum eat his dinner," commanded the king, before turning back to the queen. "So my dear, what colour roses would you like to grow in the rose garden this year?"

Millie kept quiet even though she had a thousand questions. Mr Larum might think the story about the clue in the picture was silly, but to Millie it sounded very exciting indeed!

Chapter Four

The Clue Inside the Painting

Millie fizzed with excitement as she waited for Jess in her chamber after dinner.

Steps sounded in the corridor and Jess burst in. "Can you believe it?" she said in a loud whisper. "One of the stolen pictures has a clue painted in it!"

"I know!" Millie's eyes sparkled. "It sounds so mysterious! We have to get that book about Plumchester from the library and find out more. I think we should go right now!"

"We can't," Jess told her. "King James is in the State Room with the Lord Chamberlain, and the queen's sitting in the Crimson Room. Those are the only ways to get to the library — unless we sneak through the garden and try to get in through the window."

Millie thought for a minute. "The windows are usually locked. We'd better wait until they all go to bed. Let's meet in the entrance hall at midnight!" She held out her pinkie and the girls linked their little fingers.

"See you at midnight, Double Trouble!" said Jess, grinning.

bem

Millie's mind was whirling so much that she had no problem staying awake but the

minutes seemed to tick by very slowly. The cuckoo clock downstairs chimed nine o'clock, then ten, then eleven. Millie waited until she was sure it must be nearly midnight. Then she tied her cloak over her nightie and opened her bedroom door just a little.

The corridor looked like a long, dark tunnel. Millie picked up the lamp from her bedside table and crept down the passage. Every creaky floorboard sounded loud in the silence.

Crossing the gallery, Millie went down the grand staircase to the entrance hall. Everything was strange and different in the dark. Her lamp cast a dim glow across the pictures on the walls and the eyes of the people in those paintings seemed to follow her.

Cuckoo! A little bird popped out of the

door in the clock and called twelve times. Millie's heart jumped and she smiled at herself for being startled. It was funny how spooky everything was at night.

"Millie!" Jess slipped through the doorway, a cloak tied over her nightie. "Is everyone asleep except us?"

"I think so," said Millie. "Come on – let's find that book!"

The girls crept through the State Room, past the oval table covered with maps and papers. Then they tiptoed through the king's study and opened the door to the library.

Millie raised the lamp and shone light across the enormous bookcases. Her heart sank as she realized how many shelves there were to check.

"Where should we start?" hissed Jess. "This could take hours."

"Mr Larum said the book was about the history of Plumchester," Millie whispered back. "I think the books are grouped together so we just need to find the history ones. And we need books with facts — not stories."

"I'll hold the light while you look." Jess took the lamp and held it close to the nearest shelf so that Millie could see.

They worked their way along, checking each shelf in turn. Jess even carried the wooden stepladder over and climbed it to check the highest shelves.

"*Fish and Frogs, Birds of the Sea, Butterflies* ... these are all animal books," said Millie. "I can't find history books anywhere."

"How about these?" Jess pointed to a row of old-looking books on the bottom shelf.

Millie knelt down. The covers were

worn and hard to read. "Yes, I think these are history books. There must be one about Plumchester... Here we are!" She pulled a brown book off the shelf and traced the title with her finger. "*Plumchester in the Olden Days* – that's it!" She flicked the pages open.

"It could take ages to find the part about the painting," said Jess, yawning. "I'm so tired! Maybe we should take it with us and read it in the morning."

Millie flicked the pages faster. "No, wait! I think I've found it." She started reading. "*Many years ago, King Ned was worried that there would be a war. He was afraid of what would happen if an enemy got inside Peveril Palace, so he hid most of his gold coins in a secret place. He died soon afterwards and many people believe the gold still lies in the mysterious place where it was left.*"

"Where did he hide it?" cried Jess. "What else does it say?"

Millie carried on reading. "*Stories say King Ned made Arthur Black, a famous painter, leave a clue about the hiding place in a painting with a black cat. Whoever works out the clue will discover the King's Gold.*"

"That must be why the paintings were stolen!" said Jess, excitedly. "The thief must have known about the story. They knew that a picture with a black cat shows where the King's Gold is."

"It explains why they didn't take the biggest picture," Millie said thoughtfully. "They only wanted the painting with the clue."

"But there are three paintings with a black cat and the thief stole all of them," said Jess. "So maybe..." She stopped suddenly.

Millie stared. "What is it?"

"Someone's coming!" hissed Jess, pulling Millie to her feet.

Together, they ran across the library and dived behind the leather chairs near the fireplace. The door handle creaked. Millie hurriedly grabbed the lamp and blew the candle out.

Mr Steen slipped through the door with a lamp of his own. Millie peeped round the arm of the chair. She saw the butler scan the room. Then he glided forward until he was only a few steps from their hiding place.

Millie held her breath, afraid he might hear.

"Peculiar!" he muttered to himself. "Perhaps that noise was just an owl." Then, after scanning the room once more, he turned and left.

Millie let her breath out, her heart racing.

"That was close! I wonder what he'd have said if he found us."

"He'd have made me do extra sweeping in the morning. That's for sure!" Jess dropped into one of the armchairs. "Anyway, I was thinking! There are THREE paintings showing a black cat and we don't know which one of them has the clue. The thief stole them all so I don't think he knows either."

"You're right!" Millie plonked herself in the other chair, still holding the book. "But if we figure it out, we can solve this mystery and catch the thief all in one go!"

Chapter Five

Gilbert Small Helps Out

Jess hurried back to her chamber after serving breakfast the next morning. She sat down on the comfortable bed. She loved her room at Peveril Palace, even though it was nice to stay at home in Bodkin Street now and then.

The book about Plumchester that she and Millie had found the night before was lying on her pillow. Pulling off her mob cap, she turned to the page about the painting and the hidden gold and read it all over again.

There was a knock at the door and Millie bounced in.

"It's no good!" Jess closed the book with a snap. "There's nothing in here about which of the three paintings has the clue. I've even tried to draw them but I can't remember them as well as I thought."

"I know what you mean!" agreed Millie. "They've been hanging in the banquet hall for years but I've never really stopped and looked at them properly."

"I think we should tell the grown-ups about all this," said Jess. "The palace guards will be hunting for the paintings and knowing about the clue might help."

"You're right!" sighed Millie. "Come on – Mother's still finishing her breakfast."

The girls ran up the corridor into the

banquet hall where Queen Belinda was sitting with little Prince Edward.

"Mother, we've found out something about the stolen paintings," said Millie, launching straight in. "There's a book in the library which says King Ned's gold was hidden long ago and a painting with a black cat shows where it is."

"We think that's why the paintings were stolen," added Jess.

The queen laughed. "Honestly, girls! Mr Larum explained yesterday that it's just a silly story. The palace guards are investigating the robbery and I'm sure they'll do a fine job."

"But, Mother—" began Millie.

"Now hurry along and get ready. A carriage will take you back to the artist's studio in ten minutes to have your portrait finished." Queen Belinda cut some toast into little pieces for Prince Edward. She glanced at the scarf round Millie's neck. "Make sure you wear the same dress again and please take off that scarf. We don't want that in the picture!"

"Yes, Mother." Millie stifled a sigh.

Jess said quickly, "Please could we both go to the artist's studio, Your Majesty?"

Queen Belinda smiled. "Of course! Tell Mr Steen I've given you the day off, Jess. Have a lovely time, girls!"

As soon as they'd left the banquet hall, Jess murmured, "We'll just have to look for the clue ourselves."

"It's a shame that Mr Larum said it was all nonsense." Millie pulled a face. "And what shall I do about my neck? I spent half an hour scrubbing it with soap this morning but the yellow stain's still there. It'll look awful in the painting."

"Don't worry!" Jess grinned. "We'll ask Mr Small not to show it. He's really nice!"

Jess explained to Mr Steen that she had the day off. Luckily the royal butler was too busy to mind. "Yes, off you go then!" he told her, before marching away muttering, "Now where is that gardener? It's very rude of him to disappear."

Jess wasn't sure what Mr Steen meant and she forgot all about it as she ran down the front steps to the carriage.

Millie was waiting for her. "I thought I'd bring these." She showed Jess the pencil notes she'd made the day before.

Halfway along the road to Plumchester, they passed some guards standing beside a cart piled high with big, round cheeses. A woman wearing a brown bonnet was arguing with them. "I've told you! I didn't leave the cart here," she was saying. "It was outside my shop. I was loading it up to go to the market and someone just drove it away."

The carriage rolled on past Halfpenny Square and rumbled to a stop outside Mr Small's studio in Bodkin Street. Jess jumped out and dashed into the shop with Millie right behind her. Rumble-tum came out of the back room and rubbed against Jess's legs, purring loudly.

"Morning!" boomed Gilbert Small, his eyes twinkling. "Are you looking forward to painting a jungle animal on my wall, Princess Amelia?"

Millie gazed in wonder at the walls covered with tropical trees and flowers. Jess remembered how amazed she'd felt when she'd seen the place yesterday. Suddenly she realized how strange this was. She'd come here dressed in Millie's clothes yesterday and now here she was in maid uniform.

Gilbert seemed to guess something was different. He looked from Millie to Jess and back again. "If you girls were in the same clothes you'd look just like twins." He rubbed his ginger beard, his brow wrinkling. "Except ... your eyes are a little darker than your friend's," he said to Jess. "In fact *you* look more like the girl I painted yesterday – even in a maid's dress!"

"You guessed that we swapped!" cried Jess.

Gilbert's eyes twinkled again. "As a painter I have to notice every little detail. Don't worry, your secret's safe with me. Shall we introduce ourselves properly?"

"I'm Jess!" said Jess, shaking his hand.

"And I'm Millie!" said Millie, shaking it too. "I have a yellow stain on my neck from face paints. That's why I didn't come yesterday."

"I see! I have something that might fix that." Gilbert picked up a bottle of blue liquid, shook some on to a cloth and handed it to Millie.

Millie dabbed it on to her neck and Jess watched the stain disappear. "It's completely gone," she told her friend.

"Thank you, Mr Small," said Millie.

"Call me Gilbert." The artist smiled. "Right then, shall we mix the paints before we start?"

Jess had a sudden idea. "Actually, we need your help and being good at noticing little details could come in really handy." She told him about the thief taking the royal paintings and everything they'd found out since.

Gilbert's eyebrows rose. "I hadn't heard about the robbery, but I was so busy painting yesterday that I didn't leave the studio. And you say there's a clue in one of those pictures?"

"Yes, but we don't know which one," said Millie eagerly.

"It's hard to remember them properly," Jess hesitated. "Do you think you could draw them for us?"

"I'm sure I can! I studied them carefully when I fixed the frames yesterday." Gilbert fetched some blank sheets of paper and set them on his easel. Then he picked up a pencil. "Let's see now..." He began sketching very quickly.

Jess watched in fascination as the picture took shape. Houses sprang up around the edge of a marketplace. In the middle was a tall fountain sending cascades of water into the air. A little cat sat neatly beside the fountain.

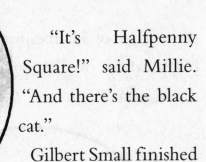

"It's Halfpenny Square!" said Millie. "And there's the black cat."

Gilbert Small finished the drawing and handed it to Jess before starting on the second one. This time he drew a massive building with more than fifty windows. A soldier in a smart uniform stood guard at the door. A little black cat sat at his feet, washing herself with her paws.

"That's the Royal Garrison where the soldiers live," said Jess.

Finally, the artist drew the third picture – a church with a tall tower standing at

the corner of Halfpenny Square. The little black cat sat on the stone steps in front of the church door.

Jess watched Gilbert draw and excitement tickled inside her stomach. One of the three pictures showed where the King's Gold was hidden. But which one?

When he was done, Gilbert Small set the three pictures side by side on his easel. "There we are – all finished."

"You drew them so quickly!" said Millie.

"I've had lots of practice," said Gilbert, with a smile. "They're not in colour, of course. But hopefully the clue you need is in there somewhere."

"Thank you!" Jess stared at the pictures. "We'll try to find it. We've solved quite a few mysteries lately."

"I see!" Gilbert's eyebrows rose. "I didn't realize you were experts. Why don't I fetch us some cake from Mr Bibby's bakery. You'll need plenty of energy for mystery solving!"

Chapter Six

The Soldiers' Parade

While Gilbert Small went to the bakery, Millie and Jess studied the three pictures carefully.

"I wish I could draw like that," sighed Millie. "He made it seem so easy."

"The little black cat looks cute," said Jess, adding quickly, "But not as cute as you, Rumble-tum!"

The ginger cat sprang on to her lap, nuzzling her arm and giving a long deep purr.

"I can't see anything that looks like a clue." Millie leaned closer to the pictures. "In stories there's an arrow that points to hidden treasure or an X to mark the spot!"

"But that's for maps, not pictures," said Jess.

"I suppose! I just thought there'd be an X or an arrow somewhere." Millie stared and stared at the drawings. There was nothing odd about Halfpenny Square or the soldiers' garrison or the church. The only thing that was the same in each painting was the little black cat.

Gilbert came back with three large cupcakes topped with sparkly pink icing.

Millie took a nibble of the icing. "Thanks, Mr Small. This is delicious!"

The artist fetched three tall glasses and poured lemonade into each one. "There you are! Now I'll work on your picture a little while you're still here." He put the princess portrait he'd begun the day before on to the easel and dipped his brush in the paint. "So have you found the clue?"

"No, I thought it might be easier to spot." Millie's forehead creased. "Of course, the thief took all three pictures. That means they don't know which one has the clue either. They'll probably search for the gold in all these places." She glanced from the picture of Halfpenny Square, to the one of the soldiers' garrison and then to the one of the church.

"Then we have to get going! We MUST find the gold before the thief does." Jess jumped up, forgetting Rumble-tum was on her lap. The ginger cat gave a grumpy meow and went to curl up by the window.

"Good luck!" Gilbert smiled as he spread paint across the paper. "And be careful."

*

Millie folded up the three pictures and gave them to Jess who put them in her apron pocket. Then they got into the royal carriage and rode towards Halfpenny Square.

"Stop here, please!" Millie called to the coachman.

The square was crowded with market stalls and people. In the centre, the fountain spouted water into the air just like it did in the picture.

Jess unfolded the drawing. "I don't think the gold will be here. There's nowhere to hide it."

"I think it'll be somewhere in the Royal Garrison," said Millie. "King Ned hid it because he thought there would be a war. He probably decided it would be safe in the garrison with all the soldiers around."

"Then let's go!" Jess leaned out of the carriage window. "Take us to the Royal Garrison, please."

"Are you sure, Miss?" The coachman raised his eyebrows.

"We're very sure!" Millie searched for a reason. "We have special royal duties there."

The carriage rolled down the street. A few minutes later it drew up outside a massive red stone building with a soldier standing guard at the entrance. The coachman jumped down and opened the door for the girls, announcing, "Princess Amelia and Miss Jess have come to perform their royal duties."

The soldier snapped his heels together and saluted. "Your Highness! I didn't realize that

66

the parade was today. I'll fetch Captain Topworth at once!" He marched inside, his arm swinging.

"What parade?" murmured Jess.

"I don't know," Millie whispered back.

The girls followed the soldier inside. A tall man with a row of medals pinned to his broad shoulders came marching down the corridor. "It's a great honour to have you here, Princess Amelia!" He bowed deeply. "I'm Captain Topworth, the commander of this garrison. I thought the parade was supposed to be next week. That must be my mistake!"

"Oh, don't worry!" Millie said quickly. "We don't have to see a parade."

"It's no trouble! We can be ready at a moment's notice." The captain took a whistle from his pocket and blew sharply three times.

The piercing noise rang in Millie's ears. At once, the sound of a hundred boots drummed on the stairs and a long stream of soldiers appeared.

"ATTEN-*SHUN!*" bellowed Captain Topworth. "We shall march for Her Royal Highness, Princess Amelia, in one minute. Everyone to the parade ground NOW*!*"

"Millie, what shall we do?" muttered Jess. "They're going to do a parade."

"It's all right!" Millie said quietly. "I'll watch the parade and keep them busy. You look around and see if there's anywhere old King Ned might have hidden the gold."

"Got it!" Jess darted away down the corridor.

Millie followed Captain Topworth into a huge courtyard where the soldiers were lining up in neat rows. Chairs were brought forward for Millie and the captain. As she sat down, Millie caught sight of Jess dashing past a window on the top floor.

"ATTEN-*SHUN!*" yelled the captain.

A hundred soldiers snapped their heels together and saluted at exactly the same time. Then the soldier on the end of each row beat a rhythm on a drum. Every soldier marched in time to the beat and they went round the parade ground, their arms swinging neatly.

Millie tapped her feet with the drum. It was amazing how the soldiers managed to stay in perfectly neat rows! She smiled as the men at the back lifted silver trumpets to their mouths and started to play a bouncy tune.

They kept on marching until Captain Topworth shouted, "HALT!" The soldiers stopped at once and the captain turned to

Millie. "Princess Amelia, would you inspect the troops?"

"Um . . . all right then!" Millie rose to her feet, a fluttering in her tummy. She'd seen her father, King James, inspect the troops once and he'd just seemed to walk and up down. She hoped she didn't do it wrong!

Trying to smile, she went over to the first line of soldiers. They saluted her and she walked along looking at the shiny gold buttons on their jackets and their smart helmets. "You all look great," she told them, wanting to giggle. "Well done."

She walked down each row, smiling and nodding. When she reached the last line, the soldiers with the trumpets struck up another tune.

Jess dashed out of the door, her cheeks flushed. "I've looked everywhere!" she whispered breathlessly. "There's nowhere to hide lots of gold. Not unless they buried it under the ground."

Millie nodded. "We need to work out the clue." She turned to Captain Topworth. "Thank you for the wonderful parade. I had a lovely time watching all the marching."

The captain bowed deeply. "It was our pleasure! As it's the first time you have inspected the troops, I'd like to award you this medal. And there's one for your friend, of course!" A soldier brought forward two round gold medals lying on a little red cushion. Each one hung on a purple ribbon and had the word *Friend* written across it. "These are Medals of Friendship as you are now friends of this garrison."

"It's beautiful!" Millie beamed, hanging the medal around her neck.

"Thank you, Captain!" Jess dropped a curtsy.

The girls returned to the carriage. As the coachman drove them away, Millie leaned out the window to wave. "Bye, Captain Topworth. Thanks for the medals!"

Chapter Seven
The Cheese Stealer

Gilbert Small was dabbing yellow paint on to his picture when Jess and Millie got back to the studio. He looked up and smiled. "Hello again! Have you had any luck with the secret clue?"

"None at all!" Millie sighed. "I don't know how we're ever going to find the royal paintings or the hidden gold."

Jess took the three drawings with the black cat out of her apron pocket and spread them on the table. "I think this is the hardest mystery we've ever had! I still can't see a clue on these pictures."

"Please turn this way a little, Princess Amelia." Gilbert swirled his brush into the golden-brown paint. "I'm adding your hair to the portrait."

While Millie sat still, Jess studied the drawings again. At last, she pushed them away. "I know! I'll go and ask Mother and Father about that cart carrying the cheese."

"The one that blocked the road when the paintings were stolen?" said Millie. "I still think that cart was put there on purpose to make the royal carriage stop and give the thief their chance."

"Exactly!" Jess nodded. "Remember that woman we saw collecting the cart? She might have seen the person who stole it from her and that'll be the same person that stole the paintings."

"That's brilliant, Jess!" cried Millie. "You go! I'll meet you back here later."

Jess ran up the cobbled street to Buttons and Bows. Her mother, who was hanging a blue satin dress in the shop window, saw her and waved.

Jess burst into the shop, making the doorbell tinkle. "Hello! Do you know anyone round here who sells cheese?"

"Well, hello to you too!" Her mother laughed. "What's all this about cheese? Are you hungry or are you fetching some for Cook Walsh?"

"Neither," Jess admitted. "Do you know anyone who takes cheese to the market on a cart?"

"Mrs Lee does. She lives in Corn Street," said Mrs Woolhead. "Would you like some tea and something to eat? I baked fresh scones this morning."

"Can I come back and eat some later?" asked Jess, dashing to the door. "There's something I have to do first."

"All right then." Her mother smiled. "Don't trip over on the cobbles."

The bell jingled again as Jess raced out of the shop. At the corner, she turned left and dashed through the twisting, turning back streets. She'd lived in Plumchester with her parents before becoming a palace maid so she knew exactly where she was going.

As soon as she turned on to Corn Street, Jess noticed the smell of cheese in the air. Halfway up the hill was a shop with a large sign which read *Mrs Lee's Fine Cheeses*. Jess was sure the place must be new as there hadn't been a cheese shop the last time she'd been here.

Knocking on the door, she went straight in. A woman in a green-and-white striped apron was carefully cutting cheese and putting it in a paper bag. A boy with a large satchel on his shoulder stood watching. The space beneath the counter was packed with great wheels of cheese from creamy-white stilton to bright golden cheddar.

"Excuse me, Mrs Lee," said Jess. "I just need to ask you something."

"Hey! I was here first." The boy swung round and Jess recognized his brown eyes and untidy hair straight away.

"Alfie!" She grinned. "I didn't know it was you."

Alfie was a delivery boy who'd helped Jess and Millie investigate the disappearance of an expensive gold silk dress only a few weeks ago. He knew a lot about what was going on in Plumchester because he went round delivering parcels all day.

"Hello, palace girl!" Alfie grinned back. "Are you here to buy cheese for the king and queen?"

"No, I'm trying to find out how three royal paintings went missing yesterday," Jess told him. "The royal carriage stopped because the street was blocked by a cheese cart and that's when the paintings were stolen."

"I heard about that!" Alfie nodded. "Everyone's been talking about it all over Plumchester."

The shopkeeper paused, her knife hovering over the cheese. "It wasn't my fault! I told the palace guards what happened. Someone drove off with my cart when I wasn't looking. They've cost me money too because a lot of cheese rolled right down the hill into the river."

Jess pulled her mob cap straight. "Did you see the person who took it? Do you know what they look like?"

"No, I don't." Mrs Lee frowned. "I only saw them from the back as they drove away. The rascal was wearing a black coat and a tall grey hat. I yelled at them but they just kept on driving."

Jess's heart thumped. There'd been a young man wearing a tall grey hat in Gilbert's shop yesterday looking at the royal paintings. Could it be the same man?

She smiled at the shopkeeper. "Thanks,

Mrs Lee. I'm really sorry about your ruined cheese."

"That's all right." Mrs Lee went back to cutting the cheese. "I hope the palace guards catch that scoundrel!"

Jess curtsied and dashed outside. Looking left and right, she scanned the street for a young man with a grey hat. There was a woman in a black bonnet holding hands with two little children. There was an old man with a white beard slowly climbing the hill. But there was no one with a grey hat at all.

"Hey!" Alfie, who'd followed Jess outside, nudged her arm. "Did you hear me? I said: what are you going to do now – search the whole of Plumchester for a man in a tall grey hat?"

"There will be dozens of hats like that, I suppose," said Jess. "But at least it's a start."

"These royal paintings must be pretty special to make you spend so much time on finding them." Alfie swung his satchel over his shoulder.

Jess hesitated. The hidden gold belonging to old King Ned was a big secret, but she trusted Alfie. "One of the paintings has a clue in it." And she explained about the King's Gold and the three paintings with the black cat.

Alfie's eyes lit up. "Hidden treasure in Plumchester! That's amazing! I'll look out for anyone in that sort of hat. Now I'd better go! Miss West at the candle makers will be cross if she doesn't get her parcel." He put on his cap before running off down the hill.

Jess headed back to Bodkin Street more slowly. Excitement tickled inside her. Everything was starting to make more sense. The man in the tall grey hat had taken the cheese cart so he *must* be the person who'd stolen the paintings too! Now all she had to do was find him.

Chapter Eight

The Man in the Tall Grey Hat

Millie glanced out of the studio window at the people walking along Bodkin Street. She wondered how Jess was getting along. Pulling her clue notebook out of her sleeve, she read through the list of people that Jess had told her about – the people who'd seen the royal paintings the day before.

Two ladies in velvet jackets. Probably friends.

An old man who can't walk very well.

A man with a grey hat.

It wasn't a very long list. Maybe when Jess came back she'd know which one they were looking for.

"Your portrait's nearly finished, Princess Amelia," said Gilbert Small, rubbing his ginger beard which was already streaked with green paint. "I just need to fill in the background. Would you like to mix some blue paint I can use for the sky?"

"Yes, please!" Millie jumped up and went to the workbench in the next room which was covered with little bottles of paint. Each bottle was labelled with a beautiful colour name from violet to aquamarine to apricot. Next to the paints was a jam jar full of brushes and a dish for mixing colours in.

Millie took the dish and poured some blue paint called cobalt in the middle.

Dabbing a brush in a pot of water, she swirled the paint round and round the dish. It looked too dark for the sky. Maybe she should add some white paint or a lighter shade of blue.

She popped her head round the doorway. "Would you like the sky to be light blue – like on a sunny day?"

"That sounds great." Gilbert was leaning close to the paper and smudging something with his finger.

Millie mixed some white paint with the cobalt, and then added a little cornflower blue on top. She loved making swirly patterns in the dish as the colours mixed together. Picking up the bowl, she went to show Gilbert her sky colour.

A shadow fell across the window as a man wearing a tall hat walked by.

Millie's breath caught in her throat. Was

that a *grey* hat? Could it be the same man that Jess saw yesterday?

"Are you all right, Princess Amelia?" Gilbert looked up. "That shade of blue is perfect."

"Oh!" Millie had almost forgotten about the dish. It tipped sideways and a huge blob of sky-blue paint dripped on to her dress. She quickly put the dish down.

Hurrying to the window, she spotted the man in the tall hat standing outside Mr Bibby's bakery. Her heart thumped faster. His hat was definitely grey.

"Would you like to get some fresh air, Princess Amelia?" boomed Gilbert. "I daresay you're tired of sitting still. I don't need you here to finish off the background, you know."

"Oh, thank you. Yes, I would!" Millie dashed to the door. "I'll be back soon."

The man in the tall grey hat was gazing

at the cakes in Mr Bibby's shop window. Millie knew this was her chance! Maybe if she followed him, she'd find the hidden gold and the missing paintings.

She walked past slowly, glancing at Grey-Hat-Man from the corner of her eye. She didn't want him to catch her watching and get suspicious.

Suddenly, she saw her own reflection in the bakery window. The beads on her purple dress were sparkling in the sunshine and the silver sash gleamed at her waist. This was the special dress that her mother had made her wear for the portrait. There was no way she could follow Grey-Hat-Man without being spotted. In this dress she'd be noticed everywhere!

The gooey blob of paint sticking to her skirt gave her an idea and she rushed across the street into Buttons and Bows.

"Hello, Amelia!" Mrs Woolhead, Jess's mother, was winding up a roll of cloth.

"Hello, Mrs Woolhead. Would you help me?" asked Millie breathlessly. "I need to clean the paint off this dress. Is there something else I could wear while it's drying?"

"Of course! I'll wash your gown for you. I'm very good at getting out stains." Mrs Woolhead took a yellow dress from the clothes rack. "In the meantime, you could put on this lovely buttercup gown."

Millie knew straight away the dress would be much too bright to wear while secretly following somebody. "Oh, I wouldn't want to get that messy! Could I borrow this?" She pulled an ordinary-looking dark blue dress from the rack.

"Are you sure? That's not really a royal dress," said Mrs Woolhead.

"It's perfect!" Millie dashed into the changing room. She wriggled out of her pretty gown and into the plain blue one in seconds. Then she tucked the Medal of Friendship inside her dress so it couldn't be seen. She was proud of it and she didn't want to lose it!

"Thanks so much for letting me borrow this dress, Mrs Woolhead." Millie rushed to the door. "I just have to do something. I'll be back soon."

Mrs Woolhead called after her. "Take care, my dear. I've made some scones if you'd like one later."

Millie stared up and down Bodkin Street. Where was Grey-Hat-Man? There he was — slipping into the alley that led to Halfpenny Square. Millie dodged through the crowd, her eyes fixed on his tall hat. In the alleyway, she had to squeeze past a boy with a dog and an old lady with a basket. By the time she reached Halfpenny Square, Grey-Hat-Man had vanished.

Running past the market stalls, Millie went straight to the fountain in the middle. She climbed on to the stone ledge and stared around the square. There were plenty of ladies in white bonnets and men in brown caps, but she couldn't see anyone in a tall grey hat. Where had he gone? Had he noticed her following?

Stepping sideways, Millie tried to get a better view of the square. Her foot missed the ledge and she wobbled, her arms spinning as she tried not to tumble into the water.

"Millie!" Jess grabbed her arm and saved her from falling. "What are you doing? I saw you standing up here and I thought you were going to jump in!"

"I saw a man in a tall grey hat and I wondered if he was the one you saw yesterday." Millie jumped to the ground. "So I followed him but I can't see him any more."

Jess's hand tightened on Millie's arm. "The man in the grey hat was the one who took the cheese cart. I just found out from the shopkeeper, Mrs Lee."

"Really?" Millie's face fell. "I wish I hadn't lost sight of him."

"But we know he was here," said Jess. "And that could be important. Let's have another look at those drawings Gilbert made for us – those copies of the stolen pictures."

"I think I left them in his studio." Millie

cast one more look around the square but there were no tall grey hats anywhere. Her tummy rumbled. "Let's go to Buttons and Bows and plan what we're going to do next. Your mother said she'd baked some scones."

When they got to Buttons and Bows, Mrs Woolhead fussed over them. She set out two stools, poured tea into china teacups and offered them a plate of cherry

scones. "The paint came out of your dress quite easily," she told Millie. "And I've hung it out to dry."

"Thank you!" Millie nibbled her scone. "Mm, this is delicious."

"Cherry scones are my favourite! We should take one to Gilbert when we're finished," said Jess, picking up a second one. "So we know we're looking for a man in a tall grey hat. We just need to work out who he is and where he's put the paintings."

Millie peered through the window. A crowd was gathering in the street. "There are a lot of people by Gilbert's studio."

"Alfie said he'd help us catch the thief," said Jess, who wasn't really listening. "I saw him at the cheese shop."

Millie put down her teacup, frowning. "There's a palace guard there too. Jess, something's happening!"

"What's that?" Jess looked surprised.

Millie rushed outside just as the palace guard called out, ordering people to stand back. She had a horrible wriggly feeling in her tummy — the kind of feeling she always got when something was wrong. The crowd in the street was growing bigger by the minute.

"Dear me, Jess!" Miss Clackton took Millie's hand, mistaking her for Jess because of her plain gown. "Have you heard the news? Isn't it awful! I was sure there must be a mistake when I found out what everyone was saying."

"What news?" asked Millie. "What's everyone saying?" But Miss Clackton had moved away amongst the crowd.

"Millie, what's going on?" Jess slipped over to Millie's side.

Millie shook her head. "I don't know.

I hope nobody's hurt."

Just then the door to the studio swung open. Gilbert Small came out with a palace guard on either side of him. They were holding his arms tightly.

Gilbert's face crumpled as he saw the waiting crowd. "I didn't do it! I promise you. I would never steal the royal paintings!"

Chapter Nine
The Little Black Cat

Jess's heart sank as the palace guards marched Gilbert Small out of his shop. The artist's beard and hands were streaked with paint and he looked confused. "I didn't take the paintings," he repeated. "I promise you I didn't."

A lump grew in Jess's throat. How could they think Gilbert was the thief? Pushing her way through the crowd, she stopped in front of the guards. "Gilbert wouldn't steal anything," she told them. "You've made a mistake!"

"Stand aside, young miss!" said a guard with a moustache. "We're taking this man to the Royal Garrison. We'll hand him over

to the soldiers as a prisoner."

"But you've got the wrong person. Mr Small was busy painting yesterday and he didn't leave the studio," said Jess. "He told me so."

"He would say that, wouldn't he?" The guard with the moustache peered at Jess. "Hold on a minute! I didn't realize it was you, Miss Jess. Now listen: we've got some information about this gentleman and that's why we're here."

"What information?" said Jess.

"It's all right, Miss Jess," said Gilbert, trying to smile. "You mustn't worry – I'll be fine."

The guard puffed out his chest. "We heard that this gentleman had something suspicious in his studio. So we came to see for ourselves and look what we found!" He pulled some paper from the pocket of his uniform. They were the drawings that Gilbert had made.

Jess gasped. "But those are copies of the missing pictures."

"Exactly!" The guard thrust the drawings into Jess's hand. "That's how we know he took the royal paintings. He must be making copies of them that he can sell to everyone."

"That's not fair!" Jess burst out. "He drew them because we asked him to." But the guards were already marching Gilbert away.

"Don't worry, Jess," Gilbert called over his shoulder. "I'll be all right."

Millie pushed her way to Jess's side. "Why won't they listen? Mr Small could never be the thief."

Jess handed her the pencil drawings. "They think these pictures are a clue. They think Gilbert has been making copies of the paintings for money."

The palace guards marched Gilbert out of Bodkin Street and the crowd of people began to scatter.

Jess swallowed. "I should never have left these pictures in the studio. If only I'd put them in my apron pocket." Tears pricked her eyes.

"It's not your fault!" Millie put an arm around her. "We can go back to Peveril Palace and explain everything. We'll make them understand!"

Jess wiped her eyes on her apron. "Look – they didn't even shut the door!" She went into the studio and stared at the painting on the easel. The girl in the picture smiled back. She had Millie's pretty purple dress but Jess's darker hazel eyes. The paint in the background was still wet where Gilbert had been working.

Smoothing the crumpled paper, Millie spread the three drawings out on the table. "If only we could *prove* Mr Small's not the thief," she muttered. "I still think we're missing something."

"There's no time!" said Jess. "Poor Gilbert's locked in the garrison and we have to free him!"

"We will!" Millie put the pictures side by side. "It's just ... there's something bothering me about these pictures. Why is there a black cat in all of them? Why was that so important?"

Jess frowned. "I don't know! It's just a cat, isn't it? It's the same in all three pictures."

Millie leaned closer and squinted at the paper. "Not exactly! This one has something on its neck." She pointed to the cat on the steps of St Anne's church.

"Let me see!" Jess leaned in and gazed

at each picture in turn. "You're right –
the cat in Halfpenny Square and the one
at the Royal Garrison aren't wearing
anything. But this one has a little
collar with a bell."

Millie picked up
the drawing of
the church.

Rumble-tum strolled out of the back room and rubbed his soft head against Jess's ankle. She crouched down to stroke his ginger fur.

"I think I remember it now – the real painting." Millie's forehead creased. "The church door was green and the stained-glass windows looked beautiful. The cat had a little golden bell around its neck."

"Do you think the bell on the collar is the clue?" said Jess. "I don't understand how it tells us where the gold is."

"I'm not sure either, but if the bell is important that means the gold could be in the church." Millie held up the drawing of St Anne's church.

Jess rubbed her eyes. She couldn't stop thinking about Gilbert being marched away by the palace guards. "Look for the gold at St Anne's if you want, but I'm not going. We've spent the whole day searching

already and the bell could mean anything."
She opened the door and walked outside
just as church bells rang out across the
rooftops.

Jess's heart leapt as she listened to the
sweet sound. Those were the bells of St
Anne's church just one street away.

That was it! That was the clue!

Spinning round, she dived back inside.
"Millie, I've got it!" she gasped. "You're
right! The black cat *is* important and the
bell on its collar is the clue."

"Really?" Millie's eyes lit up. "What does
it mean?"

Jess pulled her to the door. "Do you hear
that? The cat with the bell is on the church
picture and St Anne's has bells inside its
tower."

"Ooh, I didn't think of that!" Millie's
face flushed with excitement. "So the

gold could be hidden right up there in the bell tower and if we catch the thief trying to get it we can prove that Gilbert had nothing to do with taking the royal paintings!"

Jess was silent for a moment. "We're going to need help. You go to the church and I'll meet you there."

"Where are you going?" said Millie.

"I won't be long!" Jess called back as she hurtled out of the shop. Racing over the cobbles, she turned into the twisting back streets of Plumchester.

Chapter Ten
Climbing the Tower

Millie gazed at the church tower rising above the rooftops. Jess was right – the bell on the cat's collar had to be the clue. It must mean the King's Gold was hidden in the bell tower.

She wished Jess hadn't run off though. Jess did that sometimes. Once she got an idea into her head she had to do it straight away!

Millie swallowed. She felt nervous about

going to the church in case the Grey-Hat-Man saw her. She picked up Gilbert's cloak, which was lying over a chair, and pulled it on. She knew he wouldn't mind if she borrowed it. It was much too big but the hood would keep her face hidden.

Closing the door, she made her way down Bodkin Street into Halfpenny Square. The sun had dipped behind the rows of houses and people in the marketplace were packing up their stalls.

St Anne's church was in the corner of the square. Millie slowed down as she reached the stone steps that led up to the green church door. She could see the spot where the black cat stood in the picture – there on the very top step.

Black cats were meant to be lucky – that's what Cook Walsh always said. She wished one was here right now to bring her luck.

What was she going to do if she ran into the painting thief?

The church bells fell silent and singing began inside. Millie pulled her hood down low. She couldn't see anyone with a tall grey hat but she wanted to be extra careful.

She slipped into the shadowy church and it took a moment for her eyes to get used to the dim light. Tall round pillars stretched up to the high ceiling and the light shining through the stained-glass windows made pretty rainbow patterns on the floor. Most of the pews at the back were empty and no one looked round as Millie tiptoed inside.

The singing finished and the vicar began to speak. Millie ducked behind a pillar. She was sure there was a door that led to the bell tower. Sneaking up the side of the church, she found a little door leading to a spiral staircase. Long ropes dangled in mid-air beside the winding steps. Looking up, Millie saw them stretch through a hole in the ceiling at the very top. They must be the ropes that the bell-ringers used.

Closing the door quickly, Millie began to climb. The stairs were steep and after a while her legs began to ache. At last she reached the top and leaned against the curved stone wall, trying to get her breath back.

There was a hole in the middle of the wooden floor where the ropes dangled through. Millie gazed up at the four bronze bells high above her head. Each one hung in a frame beside a wooden wheel. They were enormous. No wonder they made such a loud sound!

She scanned the rest of the tower. Where

could the gold be hidden? There was nothing here except the bells and a bare wooden floor.

She checked everywhere and even peered inside the bells. Then she spotted some strange marks on the wall. Kneeling down, she found herself staring at a rough picture of an animal scratched on to the stone. It had a tail and pointed ears and whiskers ... it was a cat just like in the painting. That had to mean something!

Fizzing with excitement, she touched the brick. It was loose! She dug her fingers round the edge of the stone, trying to pull it free.

A strange creak broke the silence. Millie froze. What was that noise?

The creak came again, followed by a soft click. An icy prickle ran down Millie's neck. That was the door at the bottom of the stairs! But maybe it was Jess coming to help her find the King's Gold.

She crept over to look through the hole in the middle of the floor. A man in a tall grey hat was climbing the spiral staircase. Millie couldn't see his face, just the top of his hat as he came closer and closer.

Millie caught her breath. She was trapped! There was no other way out and soon the Grey-Hat-Man would reach the top and see her.

She stepped back, her heart racing. She had to do something – anything! But what?

She grabbed the nearest bell rope and tugged it hard. The bell rang out with a deep *bong*!

Footsteps quickened on the staircase.

Millie snatched the rope again and this time she kept on pulling. *Bong, bong, bong!* The bronze bell above her head tipped from side to side as the wooden wheel swung round. The sound was so loud it made Millie's head ache but she didn't dare stop ringing the bell.

No one came to the top of the staircase. At last, Millie let the bell rope go. She peeped through the hole in the floor just in time to see Grey-Hat-Man disappear through the door at the bottom.

A moment later, someone burst through the entrance. "Millie?" Jess called in a loud whisper. "Are you up there?"

"Yes, I'm here!" Millie saw Jess's face looking up at her. "I'm coming down." She ran down the spiral stairs so quickly she felt a little dizzy when she reached the bottom.

"Are you all right?" asked Jess. "Why did you ring the bell?"

"The thief was here," gasped Millie. "He

went out just before you came in. Didn't you see him?"

"No!" Jess's eyes widened. "But he can't have gone too far – come on!" Opening the door she nearly bumped into a bald-headed man in long white robes.

"Girls, I really must protest!" said the vicar. "Those bells should only be rung by proper bell-ringers."

"I'm really sorry!" said Millie. "It was an emergency and—"

"Look, Millie!" interrupted Jess. "He's by the door. Hey, stop that man!"

The Grey-Hat-Man was creeping past the pews at the back of the church. When Jess shouted, he jumped and ran for the door.

"What on earth is going on?" asked the vicar. "This is a place of prayer..."

"So sorry!" gasped Millie as Jess clutched her arm and pulled her down the aisle. The girls ran as fast as they could. Once the thief got outside he would disappear into the crowd. Then they'd never find him.

The Grey-Hat-Man slipped through the church door and slammed it shut. Jess reached the door first. "Help me, Millie! It's so heavy."

Millie grabbed the handle and together she and Jess pulled and pulled. Slowly, the church door swung open. Outside, daylight was fading.

A row of men in red uniforms stood to attention at the bottom of the church steps. Two of the soldiers were holding Grey-Hat-Man's arms firmly. Alfie was there too, grinning cheekily.

Captain Topworth stepped forward and gave a salute. "Princess Amelia! We are here to follow your royal orders. Just tell us what you'd like us to do."

Chapter Eleven
The King's Gold

Millie's tummy swooped with delight as she looked at the row of soldiers at the bottom of the church steps. At last they had the help they needed. "But how did you know where we were?" she asked the captain.

Jess nudged Millie's arm. "I found Alfie, gave him my Medal of Friendship and asked him to take a message to the Royal Garrison. Then I came back here to find you."

"I'm a fast runner, see! I got to the garrison in no time." Alfie grinned.

"When I saw this medal I knew for certain that the message was from you two girls." Captain Topworth held up Jess's medal, dangling on its purple ribbon. "I gathered my soldiers and came here straight away. We were just in time to catch the man wearing the hat described in the message. So what has this villain been up to, Princess Amelia?" He pointed to the Grey-Hat-Man.

"I think he stole the three royal paintings that went missing yesterday." Millie climbed down the church steps. Now she was closer to Grey-Hat-Man, she could see his thin mouth and his eyes shifting below the brim of his hat.

"Wait a minute!" Jess said to Grey-Hat-Man. "I'm sure I've seen you before."

"You saw him in Gilbert's studio that time," Millie reminded her.

"Yes, that's true! But I think I've seen him at the palace too." Jess gazed at the man, frowning. "I remember climbing into the carriage ready to ride into the city and. . . You were the gardener! You were standing outside looking through the window into the banquet hall, weren't you?"

"I was looking for the paintings," the man said awkwardly. "I'm Julian Black – grandson of Arthur Black."

"Arthur Black," repeated Millie. "I think I've heard of him."

"He was the famous artist who painted the pictures," said Jess. "I remember Mr Larum telling me about him."

"That's right. He was my grandfather," said Julian Black. "I took the gardening job at the palace to get a chance to look at his paintings."

Captain Topworth shook his head. "Then you admit you were planning the robbery right from the start."

"It wasn't like that!" Julian Black took off his grey hat and twisted it in his hands.

"At first I just wanted to look at the paintings."

"Then why did you change your mind and steal them?" asked Millie.

Julian Black hesitated. "I loved my grandfather very much. He talked about the paintings a great deal before he died and that made me wish I could have them – to remember him by." He swallowed, looking from Millie to Captain Topworth. "At first, I thought the tale of the clue and the treasure was just a fun story he'd told me as a boy. But the more I looked at the paintings, the more I was sure it was true. I decided I must look for the hidden treasure but I never meant anyone else to get the blame for what I'd done."

"It was very wrong of you to take the paintings," said Captain Topworth sternly.

"I hear you wasted a lot of good cheese as well."

Julian Black hung his head. "I know. I'm very sorry. I will fetch the pictures for you straight away."

"First we must make sure Gilbert Small is set free." The captain turned to Alfie. "Can you run to the garrison with another message, Alfie? Tell them the painter called Gilbert must be set free straight away."

"Yes, sir!" Alfie gave a salute and then dashed away.

"I really am very sorry," said Julian Black. "I should never have taken the paintings or looked for the gold. I thought the clue might be the little black cat in the pictures."

"It is!" said Millie excitedly. "At least I think it is. I found something really interesting just before you came into the bell tower. Follow me and I'll show you all!"

As Millie led everyone into the church, she told them the story of the King's Gold and about the book she and Jess had found in the palace library. They climbed the bell tower and crowded into the tiny room at the top.

"I found a little cat drawing scratched on to one of the stones." Millie bent down, searching for the picture. "Here it is! See – this brick is loose."

Jess knelt down beside her and the girls carefully pulled the brick out of the wall. Millie reached inside and her fingers touched something smooth.

"What is it, Millie?" cried Jess. "Can you feel the gold?"

"I'm not sure!" Millie drew out a small leather bag. She opened the drawstrings and poured five gold coins into Jess's hand.

Jess's face dropped. "Is that all there is? The story of the King's Gold made it sound as if there was more."

"Hold on!" Millie reached into the wall again. There was a hollow space behind the other bricks. She pulled out another leather purse and another and another, until there were twelve bags of gold coins altogether.

"That's quite a lot of money!" Jess stared at the coins with wide eyes. "I wonder what the king and queen will want to do with it all."

Captain Topworth commanded his soldiers to gather up the treasure and carry it down from the tower. Then Julian Black led them to his house near Halfpenny Square to collect the missing paintings.

Julian Black hung his head as he went into Peveril Palace. He explained what he'd done to King James and Queen Belinda, adding, "I'm very sorry. My grandfather was so proud that his paintings hung in the palace and I know I shouldn't have taken them."

"Indeed you shouldn't!" said the king. "You caused everyone a lot of worry."

"Come this way," said the queen in a kinder tone. "I'll show you where they used to hang and you can put them back on the wall."

While the queen took Julian Black to return the pictures, Captain Topworth ordered his soldiers to bring forward the purses of gold. "Princess Amelia and Miss Jess discovered their hiding place, Your Majesty," he told the king. "Something about a clue in one of the paintings."

"Really? Where did it come from?" King James looked astonished.

"It's King Ned's lost treasure." Millie

smoothed her untidy hair. Luckily her mother and father had been too busy to notice she was wearing a strange cloak and plain dress. "The story about the hidden gold was true! The cat in the church painting was the only one with a bell around its neck. So the bell was the clue and that led us to the bell tower."

"Goodness me!" The king's eyebrows rose. "And how much is there?"

"Twelve bags, Your Majesty," said Jess.

The king sank on to his throne, wrinkling his brow as he stared at the bags of gold. "What shall we do with it all? That's the question!"

An idea popped into Millie's head. "Father? Don't you think the gold has been hidden in Plumchester for so long that it really belongs to the people of the city, so it should be spent on things to help them?"

King James banged on the arm of his throne. "An excellent notion! It shall no longer be the King's Gold – it shall be the People's Gold instead."

Millie and Jess grinned at each other and the soldiers burst into a round of applause.

Chapter Twelve

Brushes and Paint

The next morning, after breakfast, Millie and Jess crept out of the back door, crossed the stable yard and ran down to the lake.

"I hope Gilbert wasn't too upset yesterday," said Millie, pulling her tiara straight. "Being taken away by the guards must have been horrible, especially as he knew he hadn't done anything wrong."

"It was all because he helped us by drawing those pictures too," replied Jess.

"I wish I could draw like him. I'd love to be an artist!"

"Me too!" breathed Millie. "Imagine being able to draw all day and people paying you for your pictures."

Crossing the bridge, the girls slipped through the loose railing in the palace fence and made their way into Plumchester. The early morning mist was clearing away and the market sellers were already busy in Halfpenny Square. Jess and Millie turned down Bodkin Street and tried the door of Gilbert's studio.

"It's locked!" said Millie.

"I can't see anyone inside either." Jess peered through the window. "Mr Small? Are you there?"

"What if they forgot to set him free?" Millie put a hand over her mouth.

"But Captain Topworth told Alfie to take

a message back to the Royal Garrison." Jess gazed at Millie, her insides twisting. "We have to go there and find out!"

Dashing to the end of Bodkin Street, the girls stopped to let a cart carrying piles of cheese drive by. "Woah, there!" The woman in the cart slowed the horse. "Hello! Aren't you the girl that came to my shop yesterday?"

Jess recognized Mrs Lee, the owner of *Mrs Lee's Fine Cheeses*. "Yes, that was me. I'm sorry but we've got to—"

"Hold on a minute!" Mrs Lee laughed. "I want to thank you. A gentleman came round this morning to say sorry and pay me some money for all my lost cheese. I have a feeling it has something to do with you."

"It was a mystery we were solving," explained Millie.

"Well thank you!" said Mrs Lee. "Let me know if I can ever do anything to help you."

Jess thought quickly. "Could we have a ride to the Royal Garrison? We'd be really careful not to squash any of your cheese."

Mrs Lee nodded. "Hop on! I'm already going that way."

Jess scrambled into the cart and pulled Millie up beside her. Then Mrs Lee flicked the reins and the cart rattled along. She stopped the horse when they reached the Royal Garrison and the girls thanked her and jumped down.

The soldier at the front entrance sprang to attention. "Good morning, Princess Amelia! This is a surprise! We didn't think you'd be inspecting the troops two days in a row."

Millie hurried up the steps. "I'm looking for a friend called Gilbert."

"He's very tall and he has ginger hair and a beard," added Jess.

"I don't think you should come inside the garrison right now," said the soldier. "It's just ... I'm not sure the soldiers are quite ready for a parade."

Millie stopped. "Is everything all right? Is Mr Small still here?"

The soldier nodded. "Oh yes! He's here."

"Well he shouldn't be!" Jess turned red. "He never did anything wrong and he was supposed to be set free yesterday." She dashed through the entrance and ran down the corridor. "Mr Small? Gilbert, where are you?"

"I'm here!" boomed Gilbert. "Is that you, Miss Jess?"

Jess followed the sound of his voice. Running out into the huge courtyard, she stopped so suddenly that Millie bumped into her.

More than a hundred soldiers filled the parade ground and they were all busily drawing or painting. Many were sitting on the steps at the front of the courtyard with paper on their knees. Others had brought out wooden chairs and tables to paint at. Gilbert sat in the centre surrounded by a group of soldiers who were admiring his work.

"Gilbert!" Jess rushed over, her eyes wide. "We thought you were in prison!"

"Oh no!" Gilbert smiled and waved his paintbrush merrily. "They let me go yesterday and told me they were sorry for the whole mistake. By then, I'd shown these fine soldiers my best drawing tips and they begged me to come back today and show them some more!"

"Hello, Princess Amelia and Miss Jess!" Captain Topworth marched up with a painting of the garrison under his arm. "Have you come to join us?"

"We were looking for Mr Small," explained Millie. "I didn't know you liked drawing, Captain."

The captain screwed his face up thoughtfully. "To tell you the truth, I didn't know it either. But after all that marching, painting a picture is very soothing!"

"Could we stay and do some painting too?" asked Jess.

"Of course!" The captain smiled. "Help yourselves to paper and paintbrushes."

So Jess and Millie sat down and worked very hard on their pictures. Jess painted Millie and Millie painted Jess. At last, they showed their pictures to each other.

Millie had drawn Jess pony-riding wearing

a green velvet cloak and a diamond tiara. Jess had painted Millie in a maid dress, baking a chocolate cake in the palace kitchen. The girls looked at each other and giggled.

"Let's take these back to the palace to show Cook," said Jess.

"All right then, Double Trouble!" said Millie.

Turn over for some fun puzzles and quizzes – grab a friend and play together!

Rainbow Wordsearch

Can you find the names of Gilbert Small's unique paint colours?

D	A	P	R	I	C	O	T	F	A
P	B	A	E	G	E	A	O	K	Q
C	O	B	A	L	T	D	O	P	U
O	A	E	E	P	X	E	S	W	A
T	Q	M	R	S	D	V	E	H	M
T	D	X	A	W	P	I	Z	D	A
C	O	R	N	F	L	O	W	E	R
R	U	M	O	N	S	L	E	R	I
A	T	B	H	B	S	E	V	R	N
Z	J	F	Y	F	I	T	H	I	E

★ Aquamarine   ★ Cornflower

★ Violet   ★ Cobalt   ★ Apricot

Spot the Difference

Can you use your mystery solving skills to find the five differences?

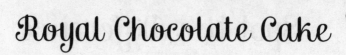

Royal Chocolate Cake

Follow Chef's secret recipe to make a delicious chocolate cake.

Ingredients

For the cake:

- 225g plain flour
- 350g caster sugar
- 85g cocoa powder
- 110g butter/margarine
- 1½ tsp baking powder
- 1½ tsp bicarbonate of soda
- 2 eggs
- 250ml milk
- 125ml vegetable oil
- 2 tsp vanilla extract
- 250ml boiling water

For the icing:

- 200g plain chocolate
- 200ml double cream
- Sprinkles

Equipment

2 x 20cm sandwich tins, mixing bowl, wooden spoon, saucepan.

- Ask a grown-up to preheat the oven to 180°C/350°F/Gas 4.
- Grease and line two 20cm/8in sandwich tins.
- For the cake, place all of the cake ingredients, except the boiling water, into a large mixing bowl. Using a wooden spoon, beat the mixture until smooth and well combined.

- Ask a grown-up to add the boiling water to the mixture, a little at a time, until smooth.
- Divide the cake batter between the sandwich tins and bake in the oven for 25-35 minutes, or until the top is firm to the touch.
- Remove the cakes from the oven and allow to cool in their tins, before icing (make sure an adult is there to do this!).
- For the chocolate icing, heat the chocolate and cream in a saucepan over a low heat until the chocolate melts.
- Remove the pan from the heat and whisk the mixture until it is smooth. Set aside to cool for 1-2 hours, or until thick enough to spread over the cake.
- To assemble the cake, run a round-bladed knife around the inside of the cake tins to loosen the cakes. Carefully remove the cakes from the tins.
- Spread a little chocolate icing over the top of one of the chocolate cakes, then carefully top with the other cake.
- Now ice the cake all over with the chocolate icing.
- Add as many sprinkles as you like, and enjoy!

You must have an adult around to help you.

Double Trouble!

Use these canvases to draw a picture of your best friend, and ask your best friend to draw one of you – just like Millie and Jess!

Here is a peek at another Tiara
Friends adventure...

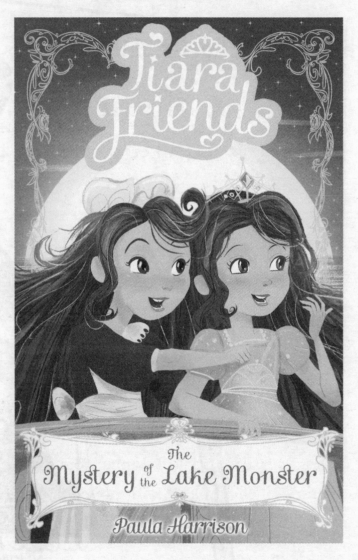

Chapter One
Jax Makes Mischief

Princess Amelia (who was called Millie, for short) raced down the servants' corridor of Peveril Palace. Her satin dress swished around her legs and her pretty yellow shoes clattered on the stone floor. "Jess!" she called. "Wait for me!"

Jess, a palace maid, swung round and grinned. She had a little white apron fastened over her black uniform and her mob cap sat crookedly on her golden-brown hair. "Quick, Millie! We have to swap before they notice we've gone."

Millie sped up, nearly skidding on the smooth floor. Steadying herself, she gazed into the kitchen where Cook Walsh was bustling around the stove. It was only two days till the Peveril Palace Festival and Cook had been working from sunrise to sunset all week baking pies and cakes for the competitions.

Millie longed to go and help but princesses weren't supposed to get their clothes covered in jam and flour. She breathed in deeply, enjoying the delicious cooking smells drifting into the passageway. "Mm, cherry pie!" she murmured.

"Come on or they'll catch us!" said Jess, laughing, and she grabbed her friend's hand. Together they ran to the end of the passage, slipped into Jess's chamber and closed the door behind them.

Jess and Millie had known each other since they were babies and they'd been best friends ever since Jess came to work as a maid at Peveril Palace.

The two girls were the same height and the same age (although Millie liked to remind Jess that she was ten days older). They both had glossy brown hair with golden tints that curled over their shoulders, and they both had rosy cheeks and hazel eyes. They were almost identical, except that Jess's eyes were slightly darker.

Leaning against the door, Millie tried to catch her breath. She and Jess had the most amazing secret: they shared clothes and swapped places with each other all the time! No one ever noticed that Jess became Millie and Millie turned into Jess because they looked so alike.

Millie smiled. Having a best friend that looked the same was Very Handy Indeed. She and Jess often swapped places to do the things they liked the most. Jess would take Millie's horse-riding lesson while Millie went to bake cakes with Cook Walsh. The kindly, grey-haired cook was the only person who knew their secret and she'd promised never to tell.

Swapping places had become extra handy because mysterious things had started happening in Plumchester. First, a crown had been stolen from the palace and then a silk dress had gone missing from Jess's parents' shop in Bodkin Street. The girls had turned detective to solve these puzzles. It had been great fun!

"We got away at last!" said Millie. "I was starting to think Mr Larum would never let me go. This morning he made me practise one hundred spellings." She pulled a face. Mr Larum, her teacher, was a kind man but he was very serious sometimes.

"Mr Steen said he doesn't want the guests to see a single speck of dust while they're here," groaned Jess. "He made me polish the candlesticks ten times!"

Mr Steen was the royal butler and liked everything to be shiny and perfect. Now that important guests had come to stay, he wanted everything even cleaner and shinier than usual.

The visiting lords and ladies had come to see the festival which was held every year on the palace lawn. In two days' time, the people of Plumchester would troop through the gates of Peveril Palace and set up stalls of fruit and vegetables as well as cakes, pies and jam. There would be games, singing and dancing too. Prizes would be given out for the very best thing on each stall. Cook Walsh was determined to win first prize for the pies and cakes of course!

Footsteps sounded in the corridor. Millie crouched down and put her eye to the keyhole. "It's Mr Steen." She watched the lanky butler prowl down the corridor in his black suit and white gloves. Every few seconds he paused and held a large round glass to his eye. "He's using his magnifying glass," she whispered. "I wonder what he's up to."

"I bet he's searching for dust," muttered Jess.

Millie put her hand over her mouth to stop a giggle escaping. At last she straightened up, her eyes sparkling. "He's gone now! Are you ready to swap?"

"Ready!" Jess nodded her head so energetically that her mob cap fell off.

Millie took off her yellow satin dress while Jess pulled off her maid uniform. Underneath they were both wearing cotton slips that looked like thin white dresses. Jess handed the maid clothes to Millie, and Millie gave the satin dress to Jess. A moment later they were wearing each other's clothes.

"Just one more thing!" Jess popped her white mob cap on Millie's head and tied up her own hair with her friend's yellow ribbon.

Millie looked in the little, square mirror that hung on the wall. No one would guess she was a princess now! "I'm going to see if Cook wants any help with those cakes."

"I'm going to visit the horses!" said Jess.

Opening the door a little, the girls peeked out. The corridor was empty.

"Meet you back here later!" Millie held out her little finger and Jess linked her pinkie with Millie's. This was their secret sign that they were best friends.

"See you later, Double Trouble!" Jess grinned before slipping out of the back door into the stable yard.

Millie hurried towards the kitchen, stopping when she heard a torrent of barking at the far end of the passage. It must be Jax, her golden cocker spaniel. Millie's heart sank. She hoped he wasn't getting into trouble again.

Holding her mob cap to her head, Millie dashed down the passageway. All the very important guests, who were staying to see the festival, were gathered in the entrance hall.

The Duke and Duchess of Sherbourne, a short couple with grey hair, were talking quietly. Lady Snood, a thin woman in a frilly dress, was checking her face in the hall mirror. Lord Dellwort, a dark-eyed man with a silky moustache, stood watching everyone.

Barking broke out again from inside the State Room.

"This dog needs proper training!" Millie heard her father, King James, say sharply. "Where is Mr Steen? Find him at once, please."

A palace guard ran out of the State Room. "Has anyone seen the butler?"

Millie hurried past him. Her father loved animals but he didn't like it when Jax got overexcited. "It's all right – I can help," she told the guard as she went inside.

King James was taking a shiny silver key out of a wooden desk. Marching across the room, he unlocked the Royal Jewel Cabinet

Cabinet and let its glass door swing open. The Jewel Cabinet was the place where all the most precious royal things were kept. The shelves were filled with masses of bracelets, tiaras, shiny goblets and crystal glasses.

Jax was gambolling round the room, his floppy ears swinging. Every now and then, he bounced up to Millie's father and gave the king's velvet robe a playful tug.

"Stop it, Jax!" Millie pulled her mob cap down low, hoping that her father wouldn't notice it was her wearing the maid dress. She caught hold of Jax. The spaniel gave a woof of delight and licked her hand.

"Oh, thank goodness!" said the king. "I've never seen him act so naughty."

"He must need a walk." Millie crouched down, rubbing Jax's fluffy coat. "I'll take him outside right now."

"It's all right, everybody!" the king called

to his guests. "Come in and I'll show you the goblet I was talking about."

The duke and duchess, Lady Snood and Lord Dellwort, trooped in. King James picked up a gleaming golden cup. "This was given to my grandfather by Queen Isidora of Plutenburg more than a hundred years ago. The gold was mined from beneath the Trummel Mountains."

"Yes, very nice!" Lady Snood dismissed the goblet with a wave of her hand. "But what's that shiny blue necklace at the back?"

"You mean this one?" King James put down the goblet and took out a beautiful blue stone shaped like a teardrop which hung from a gold chain. "This is the famous Sky Sapphire named for its wonderful light blue colour. Most sapphires

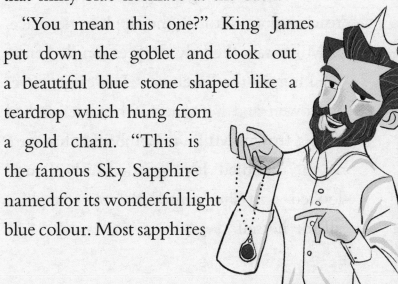

are quite a dark blue but not this one! It's the largest jewel in the whole kingdom and I gave it to Queen Belinda on our wedding day."

"What a lovely gift," said the Duchess of Sherbourne. "I bet it's worth a lot of money."

"All jewellery looks the same to me!" said Lord Dellwort, yawning.

Jax gave a short bark. Millie suddenly remembered she was supposed to be taking him for a walk, not staring at the jewel cabinet. As she hurried the spaniel out of the room, she caught sight of Lady Snood reaching out to touch the sapphire necklace.

Millie saw the lady's expression darken as the king put the jewel away. Her elegant eyes narrowed and her pale forehead scrunched into a frown. Millie remembered that stare as she bundled Jax outside. Lady Snood looked as if she wanted the Sky Sapphire all for herself.